Home in the Sky

Story and Pictures by

Jeannie Baker

2279

Greenwillow Books, New York

TO ANDREW IN ADMIRATION

This work was assisted by the Crafts
Board of the Australia Council 1982/3.

Copyright © 1984 by Jeannie Baker
All rights reserved. No part of this
book may be reproduced or utilized
in any form or by any means, electronic
or mechanical, including photocopying,
recording or by any information storage
and retrieval system without permis-
sion in writing from the Publisher,
Greenwillow Books, a division of
William Morrow & Company, Inc.,
105 Madison Ave., N.Y., N.Y. 10016.
Printed in U.S.A.   First Edition
10 9 8 7 6 5 4 3 2 1

Library of Congress Cataloging in Publication Data
Baker, Jeannie.   Home in the sky.
Summary: A pigeon with a kindly owner
and a home on the roof of a building
meets a boy who wants to keep him.
[1. Pigeons—Fiction] I. Title. PZ7.B1742Ho 1984
[E]   83-25379   ISBN 0-688-03841-7
ISBN 0-688-03842-5 (lib. bdg.)

Every day, at sunrise and sunset,
the pigeons burst into the sky.

The pigeons belong to Mike
and live on the roof
of an abandoned, burned-out building.
He built their coop from scrap lumber
found in the neighborhood.
Werewulf, Mike's dog, lives in the building
and guards the birds.

One morning, before feeding time,
Mike flies his pigeons as usual.

When Mike whistles, they know
it is time to come back for their food.
All the pigeons fly home,
except Light, who flies away.

After a while Light is very hungry.
He joins some street pigeons
who have found food.
But when Light tries to eat,
they screech, peck, and snatch
the food from him.

Light flies on....
It starts to rain.
His wings become heavy.

He flies through an open doorway.
The doors close behind him.
He is in a train.

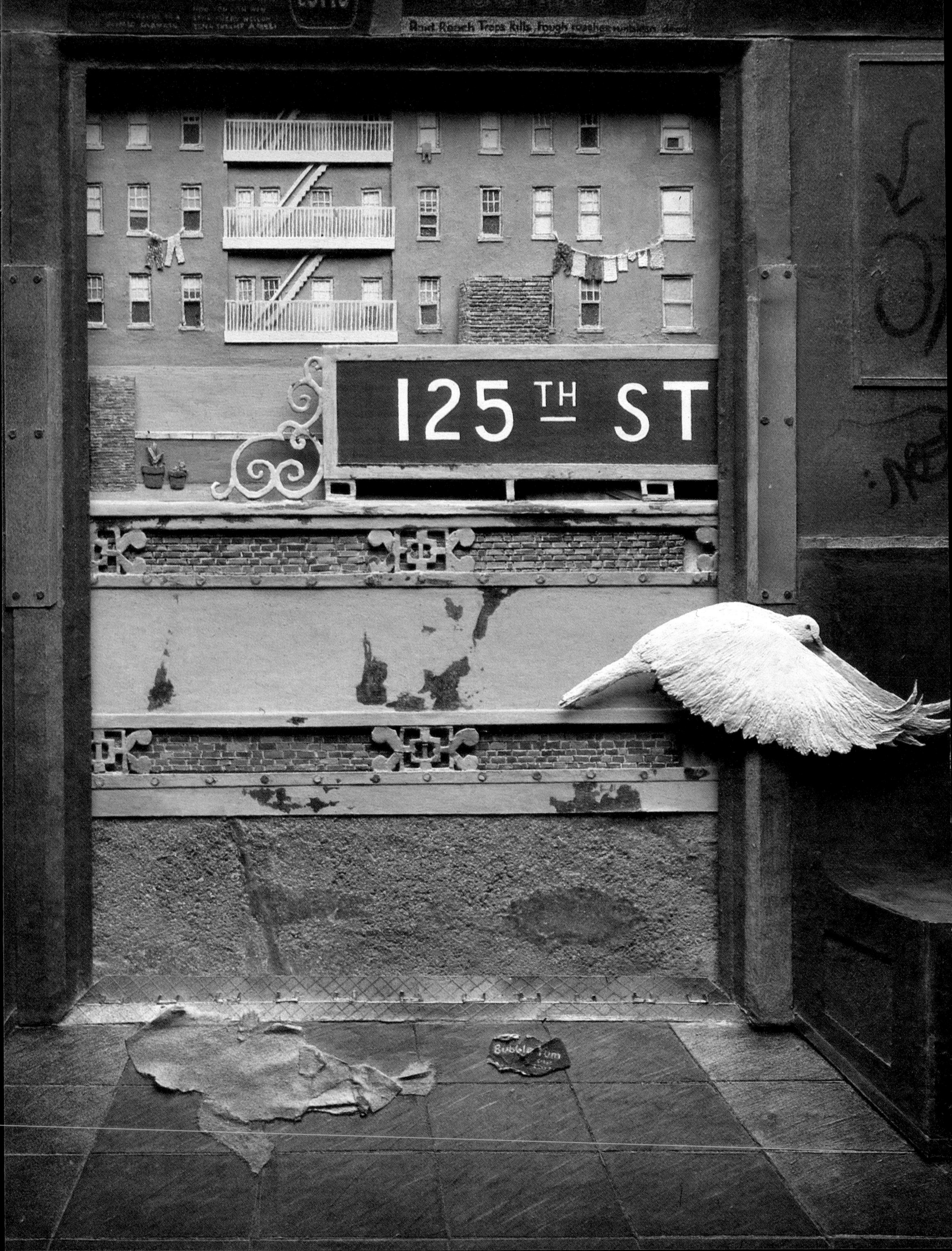
125TH ST

A boy
picks him up,
holding him
firmly so he
will feel safe,
and gently
strokes his
feathers.

The boy walks home
cuddling Light to his chest.

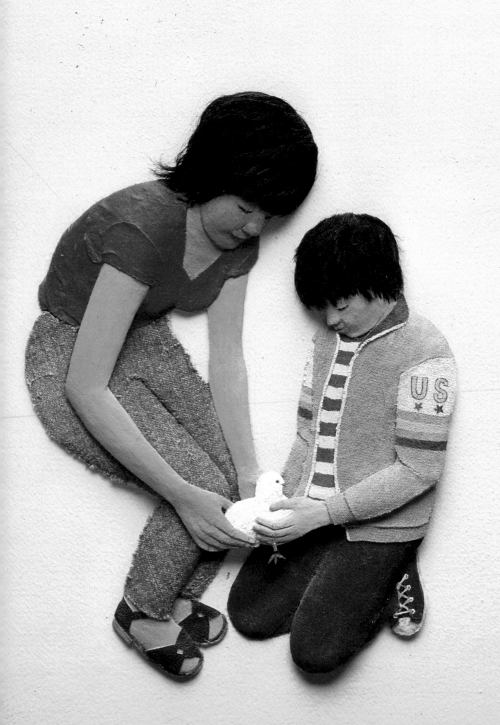

He wants to keep the pigeon,
but his mother explains
that the band around Light's leg
means that he belongs to someone.

The boy places Light
on an outside windowsill
hoping he will stay.
But Light spreads his wings
and flies away.

Instinct tells Light
where to go.
He flies high over
unfamiliar buildings.

That evening,
as Mike is feeding his pigeons,
Light lands on his shoulder
and nestles against his face.

On his roof the next morning,
the boy eyes a flock of pigeons flying
in sweeping curves across the sky.
He is sure he sees a white pigeon among them.

JEANNIE BAKER lives in Sydney, Australia. She spent ten months in New York, researching and working out the details of this book. New York's Central Park, streets, subway, buildings, and roofs are brought authentically to life in her relief illustrations. The book took her two years to complete. Dromkeen Museum of Children's Literature and Roslyn Oxley Gallery, both in Australia, and Forum Gallery in New York City exhibited the original "collage constructions."

To make the pictures, which are slightly larger than reproduced, the artist collected grasses, leaves, pigeon feathers, and any other materials that might be useful. The grasses and leaves were bleached with special chemicals and soaked in glycerine for several days. Finally, they were sprayed with oil paint as near to their natural color as could be achieved.

Tree trunks were modeled from clay, fabric was chosen and cut for the clothes, and the characters have real hair. The miniature newspapers and pieces of litter were all constructed and painted by the artist.